Aladdin
and the
Magic Lamp

©2004 Alligator Books Limited
Gadd House, Arcadia Avenue
London N3 2JU

Printed in China

L ong ago, in the faraway land of Arabia, there lived a boy named Aladdin. Aladdin lived only with his mother, who didn't have much money and so she sometimes struggled to support him.

One day, when Aladdin was playing in the town square, a stranger asked him if he would like to earn some pocket money. Aladdin jumped at the chance. Now the stranger was a magician, and for some reason he would not tell Aladdin what

the job was. He simply asked the boy to take a long walk with him. Aladdin followed, even though his mother had told him never to follow strangers. The pair travelled far outside the city gates, and then they stopped at the foot of a mountain.

The magician lit a small fire, and sprinkled on it a bag of powder from his pocket. At the same time he mumbled some magic words. The ground trembled and opened up in front of them, revealing a staircase leading down to a cave. Aladdin

couldn't believe his eyes!

"Go down," ordered the magician. "At the foot of the steps you will find an amazing garden. You'll find a lamp at the far side of the cave. Bring it to me at once." Then the magician gave the boy a ring, and wished him good luck.

Aladdin found everything as the magician had said – except for the lamp. The trees grew fruit made of gold, diamonds twinkled on the cave walls, but there was no lamp.

Suddenly, a gold-tassled carpet twinkled on the floor, then it began to float upwards! Aladdin realised that it was a magic carpet, and it seemed to want to help. The boy managed to climb up on the carpet, and it began to float towards the far corner of the cave.

Sure enough, there sat the lamp on a sharp ledge sticking out of the wall. Aladdin grabbed it straight away and ran back across the cave to the bottom of the stairs. The magician saw

him and shouted, "Hurry, Aladdin, pass me the lamp!"

Aladdin suddenly felt suspicious and frightened, and he bravely refused to give him the lamp. He began to wonder why the magician was so keen to get hold of the lamp when there were so many other riches in the cave.

The magician flew into a rage! He sprinkled more powder onto the fire and cast another spell – the stone moved back into place, trapping Aladdin inside the cave! The truth is, the evil

magician had heard stories of a lamp that would make him the most powerful man in the world. Though his magic books told him where to find it, he could only receive it from the hand of another. The magician chose poor Aladdin.

For hours Aladdin cried for help. At last he clasped his hands in prayer, and in doing so he accidentally rubbed the ring that the magician had forgotten to take back. Suddenly, a genie appeared, announcing, "I am the Slave of the Ring, and will

obey your every command."

Aladdin replied, "Get me out of this place!"

Straight away the caved opened up and Aladdin found himself outside. When he finally arrived home, he told his worried mother everything. Now as Aladdin and his mother were so poor, they decided to sell the lamp. Aladdin's mother rubbed it to wipe it clean. At that moment, another genie appeared, and asked what she would like!

Aladdin's mother fainted away, but the boy grabbed the
lamp and said, "Fetch me something to eat!" The genie returned
with masses of food.

Aladdin and his mother sat eating that entire day. But she
begged her son to sell the lamp, wanting nothing to do with
magic. Aladdin refused, and used the lamp and his ring to bring
fortune to the household – and so Aladdin and his mother lived
in great comfort for a very long time.

Years later, the ruler of Aladdin's land, the Sultan, ordered everyone to stay indoors while his daughter went to the swimming baths. Now Aladdin, who had grown into a handsome young man, longed to see her face (which was difficult as the Princess always wore a veil). On the day she was to travel, Aladdin hid behind a door and watched the Princess. She looked so beautiful that Aladdin fell in love with her at first sight.

Aladdin rushed home and told his mother of his new love. On hearing this, Aladdin's mother burst out laughing, but she obeyed her son's request to go before the Sultan and make his feelings known. She took the jewelled fruits from the enchanted garden as gifts for His Majesty.

The Sultan was truly amazed, but simply could not allow his daughter to marry a man who was not a prince. The Sultan proposed an impossible request of Aladdin, one that no man

could ever fulfil.

"Good woman, if your son is to marry my daughter, he must send forty bowls full of jewels, carried by forty slaves in splendid dress."

Aladdin's mother returned, thinking all was lost for her son. But Aladdin summoned the genie, and within seconds the slaves arrived, filling the house. Aladdin sent them to the palace, and they knelt before the Sultan as Aladdin's mother presented them.

The Sultan, stunned and impressed, gasped, "Good
woman, return and tell your son I await him with open arms!"

When Aladdin heard the news, he called the genie of the
lamp. "I want a fine suit, a horse greater than the Sultan's and
twenty slaves to attend me and my mother." It was no sooner
said than done.

Aladdin mounted his horse and passed through the
streets, the slaves scattering gold as they went. When the Sultan

saw Aladdin he embraced him and led him to a feast where the
wedding would take place that day. But Aladdin refused,
exclaiming, "I must build the Princess a palace first." He left in
haste, but not before the Princess had caught a glimpse of her
future husband. Luckily for her, she too fell in love at first
sight.

The palace was finished the very next day (with the help of
the genie of course!). So the Princess was presented to Aladdin,

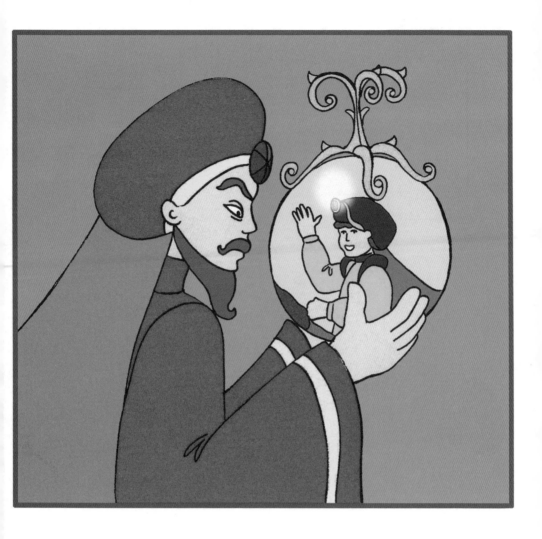

and they exchanged their vows of marriage.

As time went on Aladdin was made captain of the Sultan's armies, and he won several battles. For many years Aladdin and the Princess lived in peace and happiness.

But far away, the evil magician remembered Aladdin. With his wicked powers he discovered the boy had not perished in the cave all those years ago, but was in fact living in great honour and wealth. He knew that the boy could have achieved

this only by using the lamp.

Now Aladdin had gone hunting for the day, giving the magician lots of time to carry out an evil plan. First, he bought ten lamps from the market and put them in a basket. Then he went to the palace, crying: "New lamps for old! New lamps for old!"

The Princess heard the magician, who was pretending to be an old fool. She felt sorry for him, obeyed his request and

gave him Aladdin's lamp. Of course she had no idea of the
lamp's secret power.

The magician ran off. At nightfall, he rubbed the lamp. The
genie appeared, and at the magician's command he carried him,
Aladdin's palace, and the Princess, to a lonely place far, far away.

When Aladdin discovered his wife was missing, he went
mad with worry. He asked everyone if they had seen her, but no
one had. At the end of the day, exhausted, he came to a river

and knelt down to pray. In doing so, he rubbed the magic ring he still wore. The genie he had seen in the cave appeared, and asked Aladdin for his wish.

"Please," said Aladdin, "take me to my wife!"

Aladdin found himself beside his beloved Princess. The couple greeted each other with such love. That night, they hatched a cunning plan.

Early next morning, Aladdin sneaked out of the palace

and to the nearest market, where he bought some sleeping powder. He returned through a side entrance where the Princess met him. Next, the Princess pretended to have a change of heart. She pretended that she no longer loved Aladdin, and convinced the magician to share a pot of tea with her. When he wasn't looking, she put the sleeping powder in his cup. Within minutes, the magician fell asleep, with his tea cup still in his hand! The Princess then opened the door to Aladdin, who went to the

magician and took the lamp from his pocket. Straight away he asked the genie to take them home.

Meanwhile back home, the Sultan was staring out of his window, worrying for his daughter. Suddenly he had to rub his eyes – for there stood the palace as before! From that day on Aladdin and his wife lived in peace, never letting the lamp out of their sight!